BENVENUTO
and the CARNIVAL

Weekly Reader Children's Book Club

BENVENUTO

and the

Xerox Education Publication

XEROX

CARNIVAL

by Seymour Reit

Illustrated by Marilyn Miller

Contents

1
Trapped

Benvenuto the dragon poked his head out of his dark musty cave. He yawned and blinked his eyes. His forked tongue darted in and out. He sniffed the sweet air eagerly. After a long cold winter, spring had come at last to the Catskill Mountains.

Like all dragons, Benvenuto had slept through the winter months. And now he was good and hungry. He hiccupped, and two handsome blue smoke rings floated from his nostrils. Then he clumped out of the cave in search of breakfast.

When Benvenuto was a baby, Paolo Bruno had found him in this very same area. The little animal was alone and helpless, and Paolo had taken him to New York to live with the Bruno family. Later, when Benvenuto grew big and strong, the Brunos had brought him back to the woods. And now he was enjoying a life of freedom.

Benvenuto yawned again and stretched. The morning sun felt warm on his green scaly back, and the air hummed with the lively sounds of spring. There was the murmuring of a brook. The soft rustling of leaves. The warbling of song sparrows. The fussy droning of bees. The croaking of frogs in a pond. And the loud rumbling of Benvenuto's empty stomach.

Across a shallow stream a green hill rose steeply. Half way up this hillside, Benvenuto spied a patch of bright purple clover. His tongue flickered out and his pointed tail quivered with joy. Clover blossoms were a real treat.

Dragons don't care much for water, but Benvenuto was itching to get at the clover. So he splashed bravely across the stream and started up through the tangle of weeds and bushes.

He pushed along happily, looking forward to his meal. Then suddenly—*SLAM!*

Benvenuto looked down in surprise. A steel

8

trap, hidden in the tall grass, had snapped shut on his leg!

He tugged and tugged, but the curved jaws of the trap held him tightly. Luckily, the dragon's tough coat of scales protected him, and the trap didn't hurt. Still, he couldn't pull loose.

In growing alarm, Benvenuto tried very hard to free himself. He tried as hard as he could. He lunged and plunged. He lashed and thrashed. He tugged and twisted. But nothing worked. The steel jaws held his leg in a powerful grip which seemed to taunt him.

Benvenuto calmed down and tried to think. The trap had a thick chain on it. The chain went around a big tree, and was fastened with a heavy lock. Could he breathe flames and burn the tree down? That was a possibility. But even if he succeeded, he would start a bad forest fire. The whole hillside could go up in flames, and hundreds of tiny woodland creatures might die. He himself would be caught in the blaze. No, burning the tree wasn't a solution.

More frightened than ever, the dragon tried again to free his leg. But he couldn't—no matter how much he lunged, plunged, lashed, thrashed, tugged and twisted.

At last he sank to the ground. What a spot to be in, he thought. When the hunters came to check their trap, they might shoot him. And if the hunters *didn't* come, he might starve to death.

Suddenly Benvenuto wished he was back on Bleecker Street. Safe with Paolo and Gina and their parents. Safe in their cozy apartment. Enjoying the laughter of the children and the delicious smells of Mrs. Bruno's cooking.

In a panic, the dragon lunged again. He tugged with all his strength. But it was no use. He was trapped, all right. Trapped and helpless. A green tear rolled slowly down his long nose. What was in store for him? What would happen to him now? He had no answers at all. A moment ago he was free—now his future was clouded in mystery.

Worn out by his struggles, Benvenuto fell into a fitful doze. The long hours crawled by. Then he was awakened by noises. At the bottom of the hill, two men were shouting and crashing about. He could tell from the sounds that the men were climbing the hill. They were heading straight toward the trap. In another minute, they would find him!

Benvenuto got slowly to his feet. A growl rumbled deep in his throat. Fearful but defiant, he turned toward the sounds and waited . . .

2
A Mysterious Poster

Row, row, row your boat,
Gently down the stream ...
Merrily, merrily, merrily, merrily,
Life is but a dream!

Rolling along the highway in their rented car, the whole family joined in the singing. Papa Bruno and Gina, in the front seat, began it. And Mrs. Bruno and Paolo, sitting behind them, came in at just the right spot. They kept the song going round and round for a while, and nobody missed a word. Then Mr. Bruno started singing his part in Italian, and everyone broke up laughing.

"Papa, you're so funny," Gina said, snuggling against him. Gina, who was ten years old, got car sick on long trips. So she usually sat up front where she felt more comfortable.

Paolo, who was thirteen, sat in back with his mother. They were a little crowded because they were sharing the seat with a huge pan of homemade ravioli—a gift Mrs. Bruno was taking to her cousin in Syracuse.

The Brunos were on their way to visit Cousin Teresa for the weekend. They made this trip every year and always enjoyed it.

At Kingston, Mr. Bruno turned off the Thruway and headed out Route 28. It was a fine July morning, warm and sunny. Milky clouds hung motionless in the blue sky. Robins and meadowlarks swooped overhead. And the trees were bright with summer greenery.

Paolo leaned forward and poked his sister.

"Know where we are?" he asked.

Gina sat up and looked around. "Sure," she said. "We're right near our camp. You can see the lake through those bushes. And way over there—" she pointed a small finger toward some rolling hills "—that's where Benvenuto lives."

At the mention of their former pet, Mrs. Bruno heaved a deep sigh. "I miss Benvenuto," she said.

Mr. Bruno nodded. "Me, too. He was some terrific dragon. *Stupendo.* Really something, eh?"

14

The family fell silent as loving memories crowded in—memories of an unusual animal with beautiful green scales and gentle blue eyes. Finally Gina spoke up.

"Remember," she said, "when Paolo first brought him home from camp in a cardboard box? He was so little. Practically a baby. Not even *house*broken!"

Soon they were all busy trading "remember whens."

"Remember when he got lost and we put an ad in the paper?"

"Remember when the inspectors came to the house from the A.S.P.C.A. and Benvenuto burped smoke at them?"

"Remember when we got the summons and we thought they were going to take him away?"

"Remember when Luther Lewis made his speech in court and we won our case?"

By now, Gina was getting teary-eyed.

"I wish we could visit him," she sniffled. "Can't we go back and look for him, Papa? Just for a little while?"

Mr. Bruno frowned and shook his head. "Not a good idea. It's all finished, Gina. I couldn't even find the place where we left him.

Benvenuto was a wonderful pet, but he's free now. He's on his own. And that's that."

Mrs. Bruno agreed. "Papa's right. It's over. Benvenuto has his life—we have ours."

"Well, I guess he's happy clumping around in the woods," Paolo added. "He was getting pretty cramped in our apartment."

They drove on quietly once more, past lush farms and sleepy little Catskill towns. Then Gina leaned over and whispered something in her father's ear.

"Okay," said Mr. Bruno. "We'll stop at the next gas station."

When they pulled into the station a few minutes later, everyone got out to stretch. Gina ran to the bathroom. Paolo, clutching a quarter, raced to the soda machine.

Mr. Bruno was a great believer in fresh, healthy air. He marched up and down, waving his arms briskly and snorting with gusto.

"Breathe deep," he said to Mrs. Bruno. "Breathe deep."

Mrs. Bruno dutifully began to breathe deep.

"This is some swell air," Mr. Bruno went on, flailing his arms happily. "You don't get this type of swell air in New York City. No sir!"

"Papa, Papa! Come quick!"

They turned around, startled. Gina was at the far end of the gas station, jumping up and down and squealing with excitement.

"Mama! Paolo! *Look!*"

Everyone came running.

"What's the matter?" Mrs. Bruno asked nervously. "What's wrong?"

Gina pointed silently to a large poster on a wooden fence. The poster, tattered and peeling, had been there for quite a while. It said:

— TUPPERMAN'S TRAVELING CARNIVAL —
** Fun for young and old! **
CLOWNS! ACROBATS! RIDES! PRIZES!
GAMES OF SKILL!

Special added attraction:
THE WORLD'S ONLY DRAGON IN
CAPTIVITY! IT'S REAL! IT'S ALIVE!
IT BREATHES SMOKE AND FLAMES!

The Brunos stared at the poster. Then they looked at each other in amazement. Mr. Bruno

scratched his chin and read the words again.

" 'The world's only dragon in captivity.' You think," he said slowly, "this dragon could be our dragon?"

"It *must* be Benvenuto!" cried Paolo. "Look what it says! 'It's real! It's alive! It breathes smoke and flames!' "

"But how could he wind up in a *car*nival?" Gina said. "We left him hidden in the woods! All alone—with absolutely nobody around!"

A young man wearing overalls was working on a car motor nearby. He strolled over, curious to see what the fuss was about.

"Please, sir," Mrs. Bruno said, "can you tell us about this carnival? Is it someplace nearby?"

The mechanic wiped his hands on an oily rag. "Tupperman's? Nope. They were here for a few days last month. But they left long ago." He pointed across the highway. "They were in that empty lot, right down the road. Nothing there now but some old crates and empty beer cans."

"When they were here," Paolo asked, "did you go?"

The young man shook his head. "No, I was too busy. But my kid brother went. He won a

Navajo blanket at the bingo game."

"A blanket — my goodness!" murmured Mrs. Bruno, just a bit enviously.

"Did your brother say anything about seeing this live dragon they advertised?" asked Gina.

The young mechanic looked thoughtful. "Yeh — Jerry *did* say something about a dragon. But he didn't seem too impressed. Last year, Tupperman had a five-legged horse. Jerry liked that a lot more."

Paolo was indignant. "How can you compare a plain ordinary five-legged horse with a real dragon that breathes smoke and flames?"

"Never mind that now," said Mr. Bruno. He turned back to the young man. "Could you tell us, please, where the carnival went?"

The man shrugged. "Who knows? They could be anywhere. These small outfits come and go all summer. They play a town for a few days, then they load their trucks and take off again. Pennsylvania — Jersey — Connecticut — upstate New York — they travel all over this area. Summertime is their big season."

Mr. Bruno nodded. He thanked the young man for his help, and the family trooped slowly back to the car. Everyone was upset. On the highway once again, they talked about the disturbing poster.

"Some mess," said Mrs. Bruno.

Gina tried to look at the bright side. "We're not even sure the dragon on the poster *is* Benvenuto," she pointed out.

"I bet it is," Paolo replied anxiously. "How many dragons you think there *are* around here?"

"Maybe it's just a made-up one," his sister explained. "Maybe they took a cow and painted it green. And then stuck scales on it, cut out of tinfoil."

Paolo hooted with scorn. "Who ever heard of a dragon that gives milk and says 'Moo'?"

"Well, I only thought—"

"Moo!" said Paolo, taunting her. "Mooo-oo!"

Papa took a hand. "Everybody calm down. No more arguing and no more squabbling. It's a mystery, *si*. But we'll puzzle it out. We'll just have to find that carnival. Is not easy, but there must be a way."

Gina blinked back her tears. "Poor Benvenuto! I hate to think of him in a dumb old sideshow! I just *hate* it! What if they're mean to him? What if he's in an awful little cage? What if he's scared and hungry?"

Mrs. Bruno leaned forward and patted her daughter's shoulder. "Don't cry, *cara*. Be brave. When we get home, we'll think of something to do."

They settled down at last, and tried to enjoy the rest of the ride. But the message on the poster worried them. The morning's carefree mood melted away, and happy feelings turned to uneasy gloom. Was Benvenuto a prisoner in a carnival? And how could such a dreadful thing have happened? It was a puzzle, all right—a puzzle inside a riddle inside a mystery.

Mr. Bruno shook his head. "A strange business," he muttered, half to himself.

And the "business," though none of them knew it, would soon get a whole lot stranger.

3

Madame Olga Takes a Hand

The Brunos got back from Syracuse late Sunday night. During their visit to Cousin Teresa, they managed to put the Great Benvenuto Mystery aside. But now that they were home again, their worries returned.

Monday night, right after supper, they gathered in their small living room for a family conference.

"We have to find Tupperman's Carnival. That's the *first* thing," Paolo announced.

"But how?" Gina asked. "How do you find a carnival?"

Mr. Bruno scratched his chin. "Ha," he said. "A good question." He frowned and stared at the ceiling. As though hoping to find the answer there, spelled out in large neat letters.

Mr. Bruno worked in a big bakery uptown. He was a very good baker. He knew how to measure flour, and how to knead and roll dough. He knew how to bake corn muffins and buttermilk biscuits. He knew how to bake raisin bread and cinnamon rolls. Without half trying, he could whip up apple pies and peach pies and blueberry pies. And doughnuts and cream-puffs and pecan rings and delicious Italian pastries called *cannoli.*

He knew how to do many other things, too. How to fix flat tires. And hang pictures. And take a splinter out of Gina's finger with a needle. And carve a whistle out of cherry wood. And help Paolo with his airplane models. And repair Mrs. Bruno's broken dishes so the cracks didn't show.

But one thing he didn't know was how to find a small traveling carnival. A show like Tupperman's, the young man had said, was always on the move. There were a great many cities and towns in this part of the country. Hundreds of them, spread all over the map. And their mysterious carnival could be just about anywhere.

"*I* can't think of any answers," Mrs. Bruno said. She looked at her husband hopefully. "How about you, Salvatore? What do we do now?"

The ringing of the doorbell saved Mr. Bruno in the nick of time. Gina ran to answer it. When she saw Olga Foley standing there, she broke into a big grin.

Madame Olga, who owned a pet shop nearby, was small and round. She had orange hair and wore yards of colored beads. Last year, during Benvenuto's court hearing, Olga had been a great help. And since then, she and the Brunos had become good friends.

Everyone greeted her warmly, and Mr. Bruno offered her the best chair. Olga plunked her enormous knitting bag alongside and made herself comfortable.

"It's nice to see you," Mrs. Bruno said with a smile. "Will you have coffee?"

Madame Olga shook her head. "Not now, thanks. This isn't just a social visit, Clara. I came to help."

Mr. Bruno looked a bit puzzled. "Help how?"

"I met Paolo today, after school," Olga explained. "He told me about the poster you saw.

The one advertising the dragon. So here I am."

They stared at her, baffled, and Madame Olga grinned. "I never mentioned it to you folks before—but way back in my youth, when I was in my twenties, I worked in a carnival. I ran a mitt camp."

Gina's eyes widened. "A *what?*"

"A mitt camp, honey. 'Mitt' is an old slang word for 'hand.' I used to read palms. I also told fortunes with a special deck of cards. I still carry my fortune cards around with me. Force of habit, I guess." Olga sighed wistfully. "I had quite a set-up in those days—my own little tent, with a big oilcloth sign outside. The sign said: 'Madame Olga: Sees All, Knows All.' "

Her eyes twinkled. "My goodness, that was so long ago. I haven't thought about it in years."

"It was very nice of you to come over," Mrs. Bruno said. "Tell me, did you ever hear of Tupperman's Traveling Carnival?"

Olga's pink face was thoughtful. "Tupperman, Tupperman. There was a T.J. Tupperman working in my old outfit. Used to run the cotton candy stand. A lovely gentleman, T.J. I wonder if he could be the same man—"

"You think perhaps you can find him for

us?" asked Mr. Bruno.

"That shouldn't be hard." Olga reached into her giant knitting bag. "I brought something to show you." She rummaged around and began yanking things out. She pulled out her needle-point. And her handkerchief. And some lipsticks. And a plastic rain hat. And a large Japanese fan.

Also an ivory comb, a laundry list, a box of birdseed, a tattered address book, her fortune cards, a package of lemon sour balls, a puppy toy made of rubber and an old pair of slippers. At last she fished out a small folded newspaper and waved it happily.

"I knew it was in there somewhere!" she said. "This is the latest copy of *Billboard*. A carny can't live without this little paper."

"What's a carny?" Gina asked, growing more wide-eyed every second.

Madame Olga smiled. "It's short for carnival worker, honey. People who work in a carnival are all known as carnies."

She opened the newspaper briskly. "*Billboard* has all the carnival news. Want ads. Job openings. Equipment and props for sale. Also a complete schedule of all the traveling shows—

where they're playing, and when."

She ran a plump finger down a long list of towns and dates, while the Brunos watched anxiously.

"Here it is!" Olga cried. "Tupperman's Trav-

eling Carnival! Let's see—today's the 24th. That means—um—next weekend they'll be playing in Dover, New Jersey."

Paolo raced to his room and came back with a large atlas—a gift from his parents for his thirteenth birthday. He flipped quickly to the New Jersey map, and he and Gina hunted for Dover.

"Found it!" he shouted, and everyone crowded around for a look.

"Well, that's not far at all," Olga said. "Only about forty miles from Manhattan. You can drive out there next Saturday and see for yourself."

Mr. Bruno smiled. *"Buono*—a good idea. Renting a car is expensive, but—"

Olga Foley's eyes twinkled again. "I'll make a deal with you, Salvatore. You can use my station wagon, on one condition—I get to go with you."

"Neat!" shouted Paolo.

"Please say yes, Papa!" Gina cried.

"Of course, of course," Mr. Bruno said, beaming. *"Grazie,* Olga. Is a deal."

With matters settled, everyone felt more relaxed. Mrs. Bruno hurried into the kitchen and soon appeared with coffee and cake.

Madame Olga reloaded her knitting bag. She sat back and sipped her coffee contentedly. "It's a lucky thing," she said, "that Gina spotted that poster at the gas station. Of course, we're not even sure their dragon *is* Benvenuto. Carnies sometimes do crazy things. Who knows? They might have gotten a cow and painted it green. And then stuck scales on it, cut out of tinfoil."

Gina shot a triumphant glance at Paolo, who pretended not to notice.

"Well," Mrs. Bruno said, "next weekend we'll drive out there and get to the bottom of it."

Paolo turned to their visitor. "Can you *really* tell fortunes?" he asked.

Olga Foley smiled. "Not exactly, Paolo. I never pretended that I could see into the future, or anything like that. But I'm a good judge of character. And I can spot problems. You know, most folks—the grownups, anyway—are usually worried about *something*."

Mr. Bruno nodded. "*Si,* is true."

"Maybe it's their health," Olga went on, "or their kids, or keeping up payments on the car. You had to be a psychologist in that game; know how to size people up. I'd study their palms, or lay out my cards—then I'd tell them something *nice.* Something that would kinda give 'em a lift. I only charged a quarter, and I always gave folks their money's worth."

Paolo spoke up hesitantly. "Could you—would you—uh—get out your cards and tell Benvenuto's fortune for us?"

Olga smiled. "Don't you fall for that stuff, Paolo. It's all nonsense."

"We know that," Gina chimed in. "But won't you do it, anyway? Just for fun? *Please?*"

Urged on by the others, Olga finally agreed. "Okay," she said. "But remember—it's only pretend."

They quickly cleared a space on the coffee table, and Olga began laying out her cards. She laid them out in rows of five.

"There—see all those hearts?" she said. "Hearts stand for love. There's a lot of love around Benvenuto—" She laid down another row. "—and look at those diamonds at each end! Diamonds stand for wealth. But they can also mean big changes are coming. And now—"

Madame Olga put a single card down, right in the middle of the rows. She stared at it for a moment, and her expression changed. Then she swept all the cards into a pile and dumped them back in her knitting bag. "This is silly," she said. "Just a waste of time." She looked at her watch. "Goodness, how late it is! I'd better be running along."

Olga left in a flurry of goodbyes and hasty plans for their trip on Saturday. The Brunos were puzzled by her rather sudden departure. But they were also very excited about the weekend to come, and they didn't give Olga's behavior too much thought.

"She was probably just tired," Mr. Bruno said.

"Me, too," Mrs. Bruno said, yawning. "I don't think I'll even stay up for the ten o'clock news."

Down on Bleecker Street, Madame Olga walked slowly toward her apartment above the pet shop. Her forehead was creased in a worried frown. She never should have tried it; she should have left well enough alone. Of course, cards could *not* tell the future. It was impossible! Still, that last one, the key card—she just couldn't tell the Brunos.

Olga Foley sighed heavily. The Ace of Spades, upside down, was a frightening omen.

It stood for doom and disaster. Ridiculous, of course. Pure nonsense. Yet try as she would, she couldn't shake off her nagging fears.

The Ace of Spades, upside down. If you took the cards seriously, it could mean only one thing: *danger for Benvenuto.*

4
A Fateful Storm

The star attraction of Tupperman's Traveling Carnival blinked his blue eyes lazily. He walked to the side of his pen and scratched his green scaly back against a post.

Benvenuto the dragon—for it was indeed he—had just finished supper. And now he was ready for a nap.

Outside, Benvenuto could hear the shouts of the workmen as they set up various tents and rides. By now, these sounds were friendly and familiar to him. With a contented belch, the dragon curled up in a corner on his bed of hay. As he began to doze, he thought back over the strange events of the past few months.

So much had happened since he first caught his foot in the trap! That particular day, he recalled, the two hunters had climbed the hill and found him. They were amazed to see Benvenuto—but they didn't shoot him, as he feared. Instead they tied him up and took him to an old barn. And the next thing he knew, he had been sold to the carnival.

It had turned out much better than he expected. Most dragons take naturally to show business. And so did Benvenuto. Life in the Catskill Mountains had been pleasant—but very lonely. Now he had lots of company. And plenty of good food. And a roomy pen with a big glass window on the front. Of course, he didn't like bumping around in a truck from one place to another. But once the bumping stopped and his display was set up, he really enjoyed himself.

Many people came to see Tupperman's amazing dragon. Old folks, teen-agers, children—they all came to look and to marvel. It made Benvenuto feel useful and important. He had a good time marching up and down and showing off. Sometimes, as an extra treat, he would puff smoke for his visitors. Or even huff a few small flames.

"That dragon," Mr. Tupperman would say proudly, "has grease paint in his blood. He's a born actor."

Well, life was certainly full of wonders and surprises. Benvenuto burrowed deeper into his hay. He had to get some rest, so he would be fresh for the next show. His eyelids slowly drooped. Then, comfortable and content, he drifted off to sleep.

Meanwhile, Tobias Tupperman ("T.J." for short) stood outside his trailer and squinted up at the sky. Dark clouds were gathering. A sharp wind was beginning to blow. And he could hear thunder rumbling beyond the ridge of hills.

The carnival owner frowned. They might be in for a storm, which was too bad. Dover was a good sized town, and he knew they would draw big crowds for the weekend — *if* the weather held out.

Mr. Tupperman was a solid little man with a friendly face, merry eyes and a bushy white beard. If it weren't for his purple shirt, his sneakers and his battered straw hat, he could almost pass for Santa Claus.

As he walked along the midway, the carnival's main street, T.J.'s lively eyes darted everywhere. Around him there was noise and bustle — Tupperman's Traveling Carnival coming to life. Workmen were busy putting up tents and booths. Others were stringing colorful lights and banners. A small truck rumbled by as men spread clean yellow sawdust over the hard-packed ground. In the middle of all this, the big frame of a ferris wheel began to take shape. And the joyous sound of a calliope could be heard, as another crew set up the merry-go-round.

Mr. Tupperman glanced down the midway and smiled with satisfaction. He was glad to see that the dragon's tent was already in place. With its red and white stripes and its blue flags snapping in the breeze, it looked very festive. By golly, getting that dragon (or *whatever* it was) had been a terrific idea. The animal was a very popular exhibit. What's more he was gentle and friendly, and all the carnies loved him.

T.J. turned to a man working nearby. "Clyde," he said, "go check the dragon's pen. Make sure he has fresh water and clean hay.

And you'd better check the ropes on his tent. Be sure they're good and tight. The wind's getting worse, and I don't want any trouble." The workman nodded and hurried off.

Humming to himself, Mr. Tupperman continued his inspection tour. He strolled past the Loop-A-Hoop booth. And the popcorn and lemonade wagon. And the Dodge-'Em Car ride. And a small tent with a sign that said: "Bust The Balloons—3 Darts for 10 cents." He waved to Samson, Jr., the carnival's strong man. And to Aunt Matty, who ran the bingo game. And to Ray Rodeo, who was practicing fancy rope tricks outside the Wild West exhibit.

A tall, lanky workman came over. "T.J.," he said, "the power lines are hooked up. We'll have our lights in a few minutes."

"Fine, Barney," said Mr. Tupperman. He gazed anxiously at the sky again. "Tell the boys to put double stakes around all the main tents," he added. "Looks like we're in for rough weather."

Now the black clouds were piling up fast, the thunder grew louder, and streaks of lightning began to flash overhead.

Plop! Plop!

A few fat raindrops came splattering down. Then more began to fall. There was a sharp gust of wind, and suddenly the rain came pouring in torrents.

It felt to T.J. as though the sky itself had split wide open. Great sheets of water lashed at the carnival. The rain churned up the sawdust, and the midway soon turned to gooey mud.

Mr. Tupperman ran back and forth, giving orders. "Tear down for a blow!" he shouted.

Some of the workmen began to drop the big canvas banners and signs, to keep them from flying away. Others came running with "blow lines." These were long ropes with heavy weights on the end. The men heaved them over the tops of the tents, then tied them down tightly, to give extra protection from the gale.

Rumble! Crack!

Thunder growled. Lightning flashed. The wind raged. The canvas top of the Fun House tore loose and went sailing away. Barney the foreman came sloshing through the mud.

"The power lines are down," he shouted to T.J. "We can't get our electric lights going."

The little man nodded and wiped the rain from his face with a big red bandanna. "We'll have to use kerosene lamps," he said, "and hope for the best."

By now, Mr. Tupperman was soaked to the skin. Wearily he headed back to the trailer to change his clothes and have a cup of hot coffee.

Dry and warm at last, T.J. watched the rain pelting against the little window. Well, he'd seen storms that were a lot worse. And this one couldn't last forever. Tomorrow was Saturday. If the sun came out, they'd be able to clean everything up. Then they'd be ready in time for the evening crowds.

Crack ... CRASH!

There was another flash of lightning, followed by a terribly loud noise. To T.J., it sounded almost like a cannon shot.

He poked his head out of the trailer door.

"What in the world was *that?*" he shouted to one of the men working outside.

"A lightning bolt, T.J. It hit a big tree down at the far end! Knocked it clean over!"

Mr. Tupperman stood on tiptoes and peered through the downpour. "Oh, *no!*" he gasped.

He raced down the steps and out into the storm again.

"Clyde! Barney! Everyone come quick!" he shouted. "That tree landed right on the dragon's tent!"

When they reached the tent, they stood in the rain and stared in dismay. It was very dark, but they could see that the tree had struck the tent a glancing blow. The striped canvas top was in pieces. The blue flags were ripped and torn. The glass front was shattered.

And worst of all, there was no sign anywhere of Benvenuto.

5
Lost in the Woods

Saturday morning dawned bright and calm. The big gale was over. The sun came out again, and its warm rays spread happiness and good cheer.

But Benvenuto the dragon was in no mood to be either happy or cheerful. He had been floundering in circles all night long. For hours, he had wandered through the drenching rain. Bumping into trees. Tripping over roots. Crashing into bushes. Flopping in the mud.

The tired dragon crawled into a clump of tall weeds and sat down to rest. Well, he was in trouble now. And all because of that rotten storm.

Benvenuto had always been scared of thunder and lightning. So, when it began, he had crawled under his hay pile to hide. Then suddenly the tree came crashing down. It made the loudest noise he had ever heard. Louder than a thousand trucks back-firing. And he went into a panic. Luckily, he hadn't been hurt. But the front of his pen was smashed to bits. Benvenuto was in a daze. Without thinking, wanting only to find safety, he had rushed outside. Right out into the raging darkness.

Now, after a night of wandering, he was tired. And hungry. And lost. A few minutes ago, looking for food, he had come upon a little old lady. The lady was tending her vegetable garden. In his surprise, he had puffed some smoke, which had sent her running off, shrieking with fear. And all he'd wanted was to nibble a carrot or two.

Benvenuto got up and clumped through the woods. His feet hurt and he was getting a sick headache. He had searched and searched for the carnival, but couldn't find it anywhere. For all he knew, they would soon go off without him.

Trudging along, he thought fondly of happier times. He remembered the Brunos and their cozy home in New York. He thought of his beautiful tent on the midway. He thought of Mr. Tupperman and all the other carnies, who had been so kind. And he wondered if he would ever see them again.

Far across town, Corporal Ed Cooper was having troubles of his own. The weather had finally cleared up; but it seemed to Cooper as if all of northern New Jersey was under fifty feet of water. The phone on his desk rang steadily. Complaints poured in of highways flooded, cars abandoned, power lines down, and fallen trees blocking the back roads.

As Duty Officer for the Morris County Highway Patrol, Cooper had to enter these complaints in his log book, then try to untangle the mess. And there was plenty for him to untangle.

Ring! Rrring!

The phone started jangling again, and the Corporal reached for it with a sigh.

"Morris County Highway Patrol—Corporal Cooper speaking," he said wearily.

The woman on the other end was babbling so fast, Cooper could hardly understand her.

"Just a second, ma'am," he said soothingly.

"Could you please calm down and start over?"

The woman took a deep breath. "I said, this is Miss Hazel Whitehead speaking. I live just outside Dover, on Alton Road. A few minutes ago I went into the yard to look at my vegetable garden. I wanted to see if the storm had done much damage." She took another shaky breath. "While I was out there, I heard a rustling in the bushes. And when I turned around to look there was this *thing* staring at me!"

"Thing, ma'am?"

"Well, I don't know—it looked like some kind of giant lizard. Almost like a dragon! It had green scales and must have stood—oh, at least four feet high! It stared at me with beady little eyes and stuck out a long forked tongue. And then—" Miss Whitehead began to sob "—then it blew a big cloud of blue smoke in my face! I ran screaming back to the house, and—"

Corporal Cooper tried to calm her again. "Now, you just relax," he said. "Make yourself a cup of tea. Stay indoors for a while—and don't worry. We have some patrol cars in the area; we'll look into it right away."

He hung up, slumped over the desk, and put his forehead on his hands. Oh, brother. On television and in the movies, State Troopers were always doing exciting things. Like chasing dangerous foreign agents. Or trailing beautiful blonde diamond smugglers. But what did Ed Cooper get? He got giant lizards. With beady eyes. Puffing blue smoke. Now how was he going to put *that* in his log book?

The Corporal stood up and looked thoughtfully out the window. What could the creature be, anyway? There weren't any zoos near Dover. It might have come from the Jungle Habitat area. But Jungle Habitat was pretty far away. And they kept nice sensible animals there, like lions and giraffes and elephants. Not weird creatures that belonged back in the Stone Age.

Cooper remembered something. Wasn't there a carny outfit playing Dover this weekend? Sure, he had seen their posters. Maybe the animal belonged to *them*. With a carnival, anything could happen. He recalled, one year, when a performing chimpanzee got loose. They found him hours later, riding his little trick bicycle along Route 15. And once a whole pack of dangerous snakes had gotten away from a carny sideshow. They'd finally rounded all the snakes up, but it has caused a bad scare.

Well, maybe Miss Whitehead's big lizard was dangerous, too. It certainly *sounded* dangerous, the way she described it.

Cooper reached for his two-way radio. He would send out a general alarm. And have one of the patrol cars check out that carnival. A smoke-breathing giant reptile was nothing to take chances with. People had to be protected. He'd warn the boys to keep their eyes open — and their guns ready.

6

The Search Begins

That same morning, Olga Foley and the Brunos were on their way to Dover in the station wagon. They were hoping to get answers to their questions, and to solve the Benvenuto mystery at last.

"You think we'll find him at the carnival, Papa?" Paolo asked.

Mr. Bruno shrugged his bulky shoulders. "Who can tell? Is something we just don't know."

There were a few *other* things the seekers didn't know, either. They didn't know that Benvenuto was now wandering in the woods, lost and unhappy. And they didn't know that the State Troopers were looking for him—with orders to shoot if they had to.

"Maybe," sighed Mrs. Bruno, "this trip is just a wild goose chase."

Olga smiled. "You mean a wild *dragon* chase, Clara."

Paolo was getting anxious. "Well, what if the dragon *is* Benvenuto?" he asked. "What do we do then?"

"No use worrying," his father replied. "We'll cross that barge when we come to it."

Gina corrected him. "Bridge, Papa. We'll cross that *bridge* when we come to it."

Mr. Bruno nodded amiably. "*Si,* is what I said. We'll cross that barge when we come to it."

As they rode through New Jersey, they saw many reminders of the storm. Highway signs had been tossed over by the wind. Branches had fallen from trees. Swampy pools dotted the fields. They drove past the Passaic River, which was swollen by the rain. It rushed along, almost overflowing its banks.

"I bet the carnival had a big blow-down," Madame Olga said. She turned to Gina, sitting next to her. " 'Blow-down' is carny talk for storm damage," she explained. "In a gale, everything goes. Tents, rigging, everything."

The travelers soon reached Dover. They asked directions and found Tupperman's Carnival, which was set up in a field on the outskirts of town. Then they parked the car and started walking along the midway.

The whole area was a mess. Booths were tipped over at crazy angles. Tent flaps were torn. And banners were lying in the mud. But people were already at work, cleaning up. A small man with a white beard, wearing an old straw hat, was busily directing the repairs.

When Olga saw him, she let out a yelp of delight.

"Topsy!" she shouted.

Mr. Tupperman whirled around in surprise. He spied Madame Olga and came racing over. The two friends greeted each other with happy bear hugs and loud whoops of laughter.

"By golly!" cried Mr. Tupperman. "Nobody's called me Topsy in twenty years! You're the only one who remembers my old nickname. Now that I'm a big honcho with my own show, it's plain old T.J."

He stepped back and looked at Olga admiringly. "Well, Olly," he said, "you're just as pretty as ever."

"And you," she said with a grin, "are just as big a liar."

T.J. mopped his round face with his red bandanna. "I heard you were living in New York, down in Greenwich Village. What brings you way out here?"

"My friends and I," Olga explained, "are on a very important mission."

She introduced each of the Brunos to Mr. Tupperman, and everyone shook hands. They were anxious to ask about Benvenuto. But by now some of the other carny people had drifted over, and T.J. made more introductions.

To the wonderment of Mr. and Mrs. Bruno (and the joy of Paolo and Gina), they met Captain Sharp, the sword swallower. And Samson, Jr., the strong man. And Tiny Daisy, who weighed 412 pounds. And Marcus the Great, who was covered with marvelous tattoos. And Princess Alice, who was only 37 inches high. She and Gina (who wasn't much taller herself) took an instant liking to each other.

They also met Ray Rodeo, who ran the Wild West exhibit. Ray had his lasso with him. He

showed Paolo and Gina some fancy rope tricks.

Then Mr. Tupperman turned to Olga Foley. "What's all this about you being on an important mission?" he asked.

Madame Olga told him about the Brunos and their beloved pet. She explained that they had seen the carnival poster and wondered if it could be the same animal.

"Mr. T.J.," said Papa Bruno, who had waited patiently, "can you tell us please what your dragon looks like?"

The carnival owner scratched his white beard. He held his hand out. "Oh, I'd say he's about so high. Got soft blue eyes. Green scales. A long pointy tail. Friendly little fellow, too. And a real carny. We got him from some hunters, a few months ago."

"Does he puff blue smoke?" Paolo asked.

T.J. nodded. "He sure does. Whenever he's tired. Or hungry. And sometimes just for the fun of it."

Mrs. Bruno brought up her favorite subject. "What does he eat?" she asked.

"By golly, just about *every*thing. He's got quite an appetite." Mr. Tupperman's eyes twinkled. "Sometimes I bring him a special hot meal from our cook house. And you know what? That animal is plumb crazy about Italian food."

Paolo and Gina looked at each other.

"BENVENUTO!" they shouted, in the same breath.

"Where is he?" Paolo asked excitedly. "Can we please see him?"

"Please, Mr. Topsy," begged Gina.

A pained look crossed Tobias Tupperman's face. "Well," he said slowly, "I don't know how to tell you folks this. But—the fact of the matter is, the dragon is gone."

Olga and the Brunos looked at him in dismay, hardly able to believe their ears.

"Gone where?" Olga asked.

"*Non capisco*—I don't understand," muttered Mrs. Bruno.

"It was one of those weird accidents," said the carnival owner. "He ran away last night, during the storm. Come along and I'll show you."

The whole group walked to the far end of the midway while T.J. explained what had happened. They stared silently at the fallen tree and the wrecked tent. There was broken glass everywhere.

Mr. Tupperman shook his head sadly. "We had it fixed up real nice for him here, and he liked it a lot. Our sign maker even painted a backdrop for his pen. It had a big castle on it. And a knight in armor, riding a white horse. Looked real handsome."

"Like a scene in a fairy tale," murmured Gina.

T.J. kicked a piece of glass aside. "The way I figure," he said, "when the tree came down, it must've scared the poor little fellow out of his wits. I guess he just panicked and ran."

"Did you send someone out to hunt for him?" Olga asked.

"No, Olly. I didn't. We've been too busy cleaning up our mess. Besides, we thought he'd find his way back by himself." T.J. looked worried. "But he hasn't showed up yet—so he must be lost."

Barney, the lanky crew foreman, had joined the group at the dragon display. "Well, I know some people who are out looking for him," he said.

They turned and stared at Barney, curious.

"I didn't get a chance to tell you, T.J.," he

went on. "Some State Troopers came by in a patrol car. And they asked a lot of questions. Seems they've been getting complaints about a giant lizard loose in the area. They were very worried about it—kept calling him a 'dangerous wild animal.' "

"Benvenuto's *not* dangerous," Paolo protested. "He wouldn't hurt a fly."

"*We* know that," T.J. said, "but the State Troopers don't."

"One thing is bothering me," Barney added. "They had a couple of rifles with them."

"Rifles!" gasped Mrs. Bruno.

"You think they're going to *shoot* him?" Gina shrieked.

Barney shrugged. "They might, if they find him."

"Then why don't we find him first?" cried Paolo. "Why take any chances?"

There was a murmur from the group, and T.J. nodded in agreement. "By golly, Paolo's right. We'll have to organize our own search party—and fast."

"We can go in our station wagon," Mr. Bruno said quickly.

"And some of us can take my pick-up truck,"

Mr. Tupperman added. "Barney, you're in charge till we get back."

They hurried to the parking lot behind the row of tents. And on the way they made hasty plans.

"You folks cover the area south of here, over toward those hills," T.J. said, pointing. "We'll circle around north, through Wharton and Mount Hope."

Olga nodded. "Good idea, Topsy."

She and the Brunos piled quickly into the station wagon. Mr. Tupperman hopped into his pick-up truck, and Ray Rodeo and Samson, Jr. climbed in with him. Princess Alice demanded to go, too. They tried to argue with her, but she wouldn't take no for an answer. "I'll hardly take up any room at all," she insisted.

T.J. finally gave in. "Okay, Princess, hop aboard." He leaned out the truck window. "Stick to the back roads," he shouted to the Brunos, "and keep your eyes open. We've got to find him before those troopers do!"

"Good luck!" called Mrs. Bruno.

With a roar of motors and a screech of tires, the two cars zoomed off. And the great Benvenuto hunt was under way.

7
The River

Slowly, carefully, Benvenuto crept through the woods. His blue eyes darted this way and that. The only thing he wanted was to get back to the carnival, but he knew he had to stay away from people. For him, people meant trouble.

By nature, Benvenuto was carefree; but now he felt tired and depressed. If only he hadn't lost his head. If only he hadn't run, he would be safe with his friends on the midway.

Suddenly the dragon froze. He held his breath and listened. Was that music he heard? Yes—it was the cheery music of the carnival merry-go-round! It was coming from somewhere up ahead, and now he could hear it clearly. As he ran, the music grew louder and louder. It was a beautiful sound to Benvenuto. The good old merry-go-round! A few more minutes and he would be home, at last!

The music was coming from the other side of a thick hedge of privet. Benvenuto burst through the hedge excitedly. And stopped in disappointment. He wasn't on the carnival midway, after all, but in the parking lot of a shopping center. A girl in blue jeans was lounging against a car fender. The music was coming from her portable radio, which was turned up very loud.

Benvenuto felt terribly let down. He backed away in confusion. But not before several people saw him. The girl with the radio took one look and swallowed her bubble gum. A delivery boy took one look and dropped a box of groceries on his foot. A woman on a bicycle took one look and smacked right into an empty shopping cart. An elderly couple saw him and stopped in surprise.

"Harry," said the woman, "I'd better go see Dr. Davis. I think I need new glasses."

Her husband shrugged. "You're not seeing things. It must be some kind of publicity idea for the shopping center. But he sure looks *real*, doesn't he?"

Benvenuto ducked back into the hedge and started running through the woods. He ran and ran, trying to get as far from the shopping center as he could. He knew that his only hope was to keep out of everyone's way, until he was back with Mr. Tupperman. He didn't know that, right at that moment, Tupperman and many others were searching for him anxiously.

The woods began to thin out a little, and Benvenuto sat down to catch his breath. Ahead of him, through the trees, he saw a large open field. It was covered with neat green rows of young cabbages. The dragon's stomach rumbled. He had forgotten how hungry he was. Well, fresh cabbages were just what he needed.

Slowly, Benvenuto edged out of the woods and crept into the field. The cabbages looked delicious. But just as he was about to start eating—

Putt-putt-putt-putt ...

Benvenuto looked up in alarm. A farmer, riding a small tractor, was coming straight toward him. A big collie dog romped alongside the tractor, darting and sniffing among the cab-

bage rows.

Suddenly, the dog spied Benvenuto. His ears shot up. The hair bristled on his neck. He began barking and yelping at the top of his lungs. The farmer saw him at the same moment. He was so surprised that he lost control of his tractor. It started bouncing across the rows, backfiring loudly and squashing cabbages right and left. The dog barked. The farmer yelled. The tractor backfired. The cabbages squooshed. Benvenuto groaned.

Once more, he turned and lumbered into the woods. Good *night!* Would he *ever* get back to the carnival in one piece? This time he made a wide circle into the deepest part of the forest. And he didn't slow down until he was sure he wasn't being followed.

All this running had made Benvenuto hungrier than ever. He trudged into a grove of tall pine trees. The air was heavy with the sweet odor of pine, but Benvenuto was too hungry to enjoy it. He nibbled a few tiny mushrooms. He chewed on a bit of ivy. He munched a pine cone. None of it was very filling.

Then, deep in the grove, he came to a little picnic area. The area was deserted. There were no people around. Just some wooden tables and benches, an outdoor barbeque grill, and a large trash can.

The dragon looked at the trash can thoughtfully. His tongue darted in and out. Well, leftovers were better than nothing—this was no time to be picky.

Benvenuto crept to the trash can. He tipped it over and the soggy contents spilled out. Gratefully, he helped himself to a piece of fried chicken, a bit of onion, some potato chips (slightly stale), a morsel of hamburger (medium rare), a chunk of tomato, a slice of dill pickle, part of a chocolate eclair, and half of a perfectly good apple.

When he finished, Benvenuto sighed with relief. That was the first decent meal he'd had in a good while. Now he needed a drink of water to wash it all down.

The dragon looked around. There were a few rain puddles nearby, but they were very muddy. Searching beyond the pine grove, he came to a gulley. And at the bottom of the gulley was a river, bubbling along rapidly. Benvenuto's eyes sparkled. A cool drink of river water would really hit the spot. He would take a good long drink. Then he would curl up under some bushes for a nap. Later, when he felt rested, he would look for the carnival again.

Benvenuto clumped eagerly down to the river's edge. He slipped and slid along the bank, which was thickly grown with reeds and cattails. The dirt was soft and crumbly, and he couldn't get a foothold. Then he saw a large tree lying in the water. The tree had fallen during the gale. Its roots were tangled in the bushes, holding it against the bank.

Carefully, Benvenuto inched out on the floating tree. He leaned down and took a long refreshing drink. Ah, that tasted really good! A little farther out, he noticed that the water was clearer. And he wanted one more good swallow. So he edged out along the trunk.

And then it happened.

When Benvenuto moved farther out, his weight shifted the balance of the tree. Its roots tipped up and came loose from the bushes. And suddenly the tree drifted free.

Benvenuto saw what was happening and tried to scramble back to solid ground. But he was an instant too late. The dragon slipped and almost lost his footing. He crouched and clung tightly to the tree as it floated out into the fast-moving river.

While Benvenuto watched helplessly, the trunk drifted away from the bank. Eight feet. Ten feet. Twenty feet. Soon it was out in midstream, swept along by the swift current, with Benvenuto hanging on for dear life.

Dragons don't care for water. And few, if any, know how to swim. Benvenuto was afraid that, if he fell off, he would surely drown. Well, sooner or later the tree might be swept back to shore again. That was possible. But he couldn't do a thing to help it.

All he could do now was to hold on tight and try not to get seasick.

8
The Rapids

Down the river they sailed — one floating tree and one unwilling passenger. Benvenuto made himself stay calm. The tree was big and solid and not likely to roll over. He would simply have to hang on to it and be patient.

Moments later he heard a strange sound. It was a dull booming noise, unlike anything he had ever heard before. The booming sound was faint, but slowly it grew louder. Curious, he raised his head and squinted his eyes to see. Then he felt a wave of terror.

There were dangerous rapids ahead!

Benvenuto's heart sank. The river, churned and swollen by the rain, was rushing toward a waterfall. Soon he could see lashing waves. And foaming white caps. And sharp jagged rocks. The river broke against these rocks and raced on.

The booming sound grew much louder. The waves pounded noisily. The tree moved faster and faster toward the falls. Caught in a whirlpool, it began to spin around and around. Benvenuto clung to the tree trunk with his sharp claws. The spinning made him very dizzy. This is it, he thought unhappily. This is the end. Doom and disaster. I'm finished. Done. Washed up. Wiped out. The frightened animal closed his eyes and held his breath.

BUMP!

Benvenuto opened one eye carefully and looked around. The tree trunk had come to rest against a large boulder. It was wedged against the boulder, which was right on the edge of the roaring falls.

The dragon sighed with relief. He was safe — but only for an instant. At any moment, the tree could float loose and slide right over the edge. The trunk wobbled as waves rushed past. Benvenuto tried to climb up on the boulder, but it was wet and slippery, and he almost landed in the water. He clung to his tree again,

hardly daring to breathe.

Bump! Splash!

The tree shifted a little. It was balancing by a hair. Any second, it might tip over and go crashing to the bottom. And when it did, Benvenuto would surely go with it.

9

A Surprising Signal

Ed Cooper pressed the button on his two-way radio. "Headquarters to Car 18 . . . Headquarters to Car 18 . . . Come in, 18 . . ."

"Car 18 to Headquarters . . . What's up, Ed?"

Corporal Cooper recognized the voice of Wally Huff, one of the State Troopers out on patrol. "Wally," he said into his microphone, "what's happening with that big lizard? You and Ralph having any luck?"

"Not so far, Ed. We checked with the carnival. The animal belongs to them, all right. Just as you figured. It got loose last night and they haven't seen it since."

Cooper frowned. "Well, it's causing a lot of

headaches. I just got another report. It was seen around that new shopping center off Route 46. Over near Indian Lake. And a farmer in that same area saw it in his field. The poor guy almost fainted."

"Did the lizard go after him?" Wally asked.

"No. But if it *does* attack anyone, we'll have a real mess. You and Ralph get right over there. Keep your eyes open—and be ready for trouble."

"Roger—we're on our way."

The radio clicked as the Trooper signed off.

Meanwhile, the other search parties had also been busy. In their station wagon, Olga and the Brunos bumped and jounced over the narrow country roads. Every few minutes they stopped the car. Then everyone got out and tramped back and forth through the woods and fields.

"Benvenuto!" Paolo shouted. "Here, boy!"

"Benvenuto!" Gina chimed in, calling as loudly as she could. "Where are you? It's *us!*"

They searched near and far. They searched high and low. They looked behind rocks. They peered under bushes. They peeked into caves. But they couldn't find Benvenuto anywhere.

North of town, the Tupperman party was having similar bad luck. They rode along for miles, stopping and calling. T.J.'s truck had four-wheel drive, so he finally left the road and went bouncing right across the countryside. Now and then, the wheels bogged down in the soft dirt. When that happened, Samson, Jr. hopped out and raced around to the back. He put his powerful shoulders against the tailgate, gave a mighty shove, and off they would go again. But it was no use. They looked everywhere. They searched long and hard. But there was no sign of the missing dragon.

Later, as they had planned, the two groups met at a cross-roads east of Dover. Everyone was worn out and discouraged. Paolo's jacket was ripped, and Gina had a blister on her foot.

"We yelled our heads off," Madame Olga said wearily.

"So did we," said Princess Alice in a weak voice. "I hollered so much, my throat is hoarse."

"Gargle when you get home," said Mrs. Bruno.

"I don't understand," Paolo grumbled unhappily. "Remember when Benvenuto got lost in our neighborhood? He found his way back okay—all by himself. So why can't he do that here?"

"New York is different," Gina said. "In New York, the streets all have numbers. And so do the houses."

Paolo stared at his sister with disdain. But he was so tired, he didn't even bother to answer.

"What happens now, T.J.?" Ray Rodeo asked. "You think the State Troopers are still hunting for him?"

Mr. Tupperman shrugged. "I don't know, Ray. When we get back, I'll check with their headquarters. But there's nothing more we can do here." He looked at his watch. "It's getting late, and we've got a show to put on. I'm sorry, but we can't stay out any longer. We have to get back to the carnival."

Mr. Bruno nodded in agreement. Hours ago, they had stopped for hamburgers at a road-stand. But the long afternoon was drawing to a close. It was time to think of home and rest and a hot dinner.

"*Si*," said. "We did all we can. And everyone is tired. Now I think we go back to Bleecker

Street."

"But what about Benvenuto?" Gina wailed.

"Dont' be upset, Gina," her mother said. "He'll probably be all right. After all, he's used to being on his own." She tried to sound cheerful, but they knew from her voice that she was worried, too.

Silently, sadly, the searchers turned back toward their cars. They moved wearily, and a heavy air of defeat hung over them. Mr. Bruno muttered to himself. Gina sniffled. T.J. blew his nose loudly in his red bandanna. It was over, now. Benvenuto was gone. All their efforts had been in vain. And all their hopes had come to nothing.

Suddenly Mr. Bruno gripped his wife's arm and pointed.

"Clara — *look!*" he gasped.

Everyone turned to follow his pointing finger. There, rising high in the air, were little puffs of blue smoke! The puffs rose quickly, one after the other. They formed a neat line that went straight up into the summery sky.

They all stared in amazement.

"It's Benvenuto!" Paolo shouted. "He's sending up smoke signals! Just like the Indians used

to do!"

Tupperman nodded. "By golly, you're right! It's a distress call!" He shaded his eyes and squinted carefully. "I know this area well. The smoke's coming from the river—just beyond those woods. Come on, let's get going!"

The two groups raced back to the cars, with everyone talking at once. They hopped in quickly and drove off. Ahead of them, the little blue puffs hung in the air, like a silent plea for help.

10
Rescued

With T.J. leading the way, the searchers rushed toward Benvenuto's smoke signals. The cars turned off the main road onto a weed-covered trail. They bumped along past the pine grove and the picnic area, and came to a clearing surrounded by hedges. The clearing sloped gently to the river's edge.

The cars jolted to a stop. Everyone piled out and raced down to the bank.

"There he is!" Paolo shouted, jumping up and down in a frenzy of excitement. "We found him! We found Benvenuto!"

From the high river bank, they could take in the whole strange scene.

There was the dragon, clinging to his tree trunk.

There was the tree trunk, balanced against the boulder.

There was the boulder, on the edge of a roaring waterfall.

Benvenuto saw the rescuers and blinked his eyes happily. His signals had been seen — his friends had come at last! Just then the tree lurched. It wobbled and almost slipped over the edge. The dragon held on tightly, his heart pounding.

"He's in some spot," T.J. gasped. "That tree can go over any second!"

"We have to work fast," Olga said. "You think somebody can swim out and bring him in?"

Samson, Jr. shook his head. "Impossible. Not with that current. I'm a strong swimmer, but I couldn't fight the pull. I'd be swept over the falls before I got halfway there."

"We can make a human chain!" cried Gina. "Or ask the Troopers to bring a helicopter!" But even *she* sensed that her solutions weren't workable.

"What*ever* we do," T.J. said, "we'd better do

it quick."

They looked at each other unhappily. They had found their dragon, and now they couldn't rescue him. Were they going to be defeated? With success so near, would they be cheated at the last minute? It was almost more than they could bear.

Mrs. Bruno had an idea. "Mr. Ray," she said, turning to the performer. "Did you bring your lasso rope?"

Ray Rodeo grinned. "Of course—that's the answer! It's in the truck!"

He hurried to the pick-up truck and came racing back with his coil of stout rope.

"The tree is pretty far away," Mr. Tupperman said. "You really think you can rope it?"

Ray shrugged. "It's a long throw. But there's no wind. And I have plenty of clear space. We'll just have to try."

The expert looked across the water and studied the floating tree. There were some thick roots growing from the end. One clump of roots stuck straight up in the air. It would make a good target.

"Give him room, everybody," Mr. Bruno said.

They stepped back as Ray shook out his rope. He formed a loop at one end, about three feet across. Then he crouched and dipped the loop in the water.

"This will add a little more weight to it," he explained to Gina and Paolo.

Crack! Bump!

Out on the river, the trunk shuddered and shook. Benvenuto was getting weak. He watched the group on the bank. His tail wagged feebly, and his eyes had a pleading look.

Ray Rodeo stood up. "Here goes," he said. He swung the rope slowly over his head. The loop whirled round and round, forming a big circle in mid-air. At just the right moment, Ray let it fly.

Plunk! The rope landed in the water, a few inches away from the tree. Everyone groaned.

Ray pulled the rope in quickly and formed another loop. He narrowed his eyes. He judged the distance carefully. He whirled the lasso and sent it sailing through the air.

Splash! Another near miss.

The group watched tensely, nervously. Mrs. Bruno bit her lip. Princess Alice crossed her fingers. Mr. Bruno scratched his chin. T.J.

twisted his bandanna in anxious hands.

Ray shifted his feet to get in a better position. He studied the tree silently. He swung the lasso. It whirled and hummed. Then he sent it spinning.

Plop! The loop settled neatly around the clump of roots!

Everyone cheered wildly as Ray pulled the loop tight and hauled in the extra slack.

"Keep that rope taut," T.J. yelled, "while I get the truck around in place!"

He hopped on the seat, started the engine, and backed carefully toward the bank. To keep clear of the waterfall, they would have to pull the tree away at a sharp angle. He kept the truck facing up the slope, with the motor running. Then Ray and Samson, Jr. tied the rope tightly around the rear axle.

"All set!" Ray shouted. "Start hauling!"

Mr. Tupperman shifted into first gear.

Whirrr ... whirrr ...

The truck wheels turned in the soft ground. But the truck didn't move. The wheels spun around, sinking in deeper and deeper.

"We need stuff to wedge under those wheels!" Olga cried.

They all scattered into the underbrush and came running back with rocks and branches. Quickly, they wedged them under the rear wheels of the truck. Princess Alice, who was the smallest, even crawled underneath to help fit it in.

At last they signalled T.J.—and he started forward again.

WHIRRRRRR . . .

The wheels almost caught. Almost—but not quite. They began to spin again, pushing the rocks and branches down into the dirt.

Olga groaned. Their plan wasn't going to work!

Suddenly Samson, Jr. flung himself against the back of the truck. His powerful muscles bulged as he strained to push. The others rushed to help him.

"Be careful of those wheels!" Mrs. Bruno shouted to Paolo and Gina. Then she, too, flung herself into the struggle. As the engine raced and the tires whined, they shoved. They strained. They pushed with all their strength.

"Push!" Mr. Bruno gasped. "Push!"

Slowly, slowly, the wheels began to grab. The truck groaned forward. It went a little faster—

then faster still—and suddenly it was rolling up the sloping ground.

The tree, yanked by the strong rope, slid free of the boulder. For a moment it skirted the edge of the waterfall. Then it glided swiftly toward the waiting group. With a bump, the tree reached the river bank. And Benvenuto, weak and wobbly, was helped onto solid ground. He looked at them happily and thumped his tail in gratitude.

With Benvenuto safe at last, everybody went wild. T.J. hugged Olga Foley. Princess Alice hugged Samson, Jr. Paolo hugged Benvenuto. Gina hugged her father. Ray Rodeo grabbed Mrs. Bruno and whirled her around in a little dance, which left her beaming with pleasure.

"Three cheers for Ray and his lasso!" shouted Paolo.

"Three cheers for Mama, who thought of it!" shouted Gina.

"Three cheers for Mr. Bruno, who saw the smoke signals!" shouted Olga.

"And three cheers for Benvenuto, who *made* them!" shouted Princess Alice.

Madame Olga thought of something else. "T.J., what about those State Troopers?"

Mr. Tupperman smiled. "No problem, Olly. I'll clear it up with them when we get back. The carnival has an official license to keep wild animals. Now that we've found Benvenuto, the problem is settled. The highway patrol people have other things to worry about; they'll be very glad that this is over."

He looked at his watch again. "Well, let's load Benvenuto on the truck and get back to our carnival. We've got a lot of work to do—and we're all finished here."

Mr. Bruno cleared his throat. "Not quite, Mr. Tupperman," he said in a quiet, firm voice. "Not quite finished."

They turned and looked at Mr. Bruno in surprise.

11
Benvenuto Decides

T.J. smiled at Mr. Bruno. He was a bit puzzled. "*What* isn't quite finished, Salvatore? What do you mean?"

"Benvenuto is our pet," Mr. Bruno said. "Paolo found him when he was a baby. We nursed him. We cared for him. Later, we set him free in the mountains. Now we will take him back there."

Mr. Tupperman's bushy white eyebrows shot up. "Take him *back?* But he's part of our show! He's a carny now—and we need him!"

Mr. Bruno shook his head. "A dragon doesn't belong in a carnival. Is not a healthy life. He should be in the woods."

"Salvatore is right," Mrs. Bruno said, taking

her husband's side in the dispute. "Benvenuto is a wild animal. And wild animals have to be free."

"Listen, folks," T.J. explained, "we put a lot of time and work into that dragon display. He's important to us. He likes being with us. We *can't* just let him go."

"I agree," Ray Rodeo chimed in. "When he was on his own, he got into trouble. At least we can take good care of him."

"You're being selfish," Olga said. "The carnival can manage very well without Benvenuto. He deserves his freedom."

The two groups glared at each other. Paolo, Gina, their parents and Olga on one side—T.J. and the carnies on the other. They were facing a showdown, and the air grew tense.

T.J. frowned. "Listen to me, Olly. He's a lot better off with us. He needs people to look after him. He was happy in the carnival."

"He was happy in the woods, too."

"Carnival!"

"Woods!"

"CARNIVAL!"

"WOODS!"

The argument grew heated. And all the

while, nobody paid a bit of attention to Benvenuto himself. Finally the dragon went into action. He filled his lungs with air and lifted his head —

Whooosh!

A bright jet of flame shot from his nostrils. It flared neatly between the two groups. The squabblers were taken aback. They stopped shouting and gaped at him.

When everyone was quiet, Benvenuto walked over to the Brunos. He rubbed himself against each of them. He looked at them lovingly (but sadly), and seemed to move his head from side to side. Next he walked over to T.J. and the carnies. He circled the group several times. Then he pushed his way in, and sat down right in their midst. He thumped his scaly tail and his eyes sparkled happily.

They looked at each other in amazement.

"By golly!" said T.J. "Bygollybygollybygolly!"

"Well, he's some dragon," said Olga slowly. "I guess the argument is finally settled."

Mr. Bruno smiled. "*Si*. Is settled, all right. Benvenuto has made his choice."

12
Home Again

"**I** never had so much excitement in my whole life," Mrs. Bruno said. "It's been *some* day."

Olga nodded. "It sure has been, Clara. I'm pooped. Tomorrow I'm going to sleep till noon."

Madame Olga and the Brunos were on their way home at last. They had spent the evening at the carnival as guests of Mr. Tupperman. First they had dinner in the cook house, with the other carnies. Benvenuto had a hot meal, too. Then he went off for a much needed rest. Later, they strolled along the midway, enjoying the colorful sights and sounds.

"Nobody pays for a thing tonight," T.J. said.

"It's all on the house."

Everyone had a fine time. They ate popcorn and cotton candy. They tried the games of skill. Paolo and Gina went into the Fun House. They rode the ferris wheel (twice) and the merry-go-round (three times). Mr. Bruno won a box of candy at the Baseball Pitch. Gina won a large stuffed animal at the Wheel of Fortune.

And when they finally left, their new friends gathered in the parking lot to say goodbye and start them on their way.

Gina's stuffed animal was covered in bright green velvet. It looked a little like a dinosaur, a little like a lizard, and—if you squinted your eyes—a little like a dragon.

"I'm going to call him 'Benvenuto the Second,'" she announced, snuggling drowsily next to her father.

As they drove along, Paolo was thoughtful. "There's one thing I still can't figure out," he said. "How come Benvenuto decided to stay with the carnival? Wouldn't he be happier living his own life? And being his own boss?"

"It's not too hard to understand, Paolo," Olga answered. "Benvenuto isn't a loner; he really needs company. And another thing—well, think for a minute about those strange people in the carny. Tiny Daisy, who weighs over 400 pounds. And Marcus the Great, all covered with tattoos. And Princess Alice, who's only three feet tall. People like that haven't got it easy. They just don't fit into the ordinary world. And neither does a smoke-breathing dragon. So they've made their *own* little world. A carnival is a place where they're accepted. They can be happy together — and make a lot of other folks happy, too."

Mr. Bruno nodded and yawned. "Is true. Benvenuto has a good home now. A place where he fits in."

"And friends to be with," Mrs. Bruno added. "That's the most important part."

They drove on in silence, lost in thought. So many marvelous things had happened! And now they had a whole new set of memories to keep and to treasure.

Memories are a bond. They bring people closer together. As the weeks and months rolled by, Olga and the Brunos would unfold these new treasures, one by one. They would share their recollections often with one another. As time passed, each exciting moment would be lovingly examined. And discussed.

And compared. And thought about. And lived all over again.

Paolo grinned. "Remember when Ray lassoed that old tree at the very last minute? Boy, was I excited!"

"Remember," said Mrs. Bruno, "when we all helped Samson, Jr. push the truck up the hill? *That* was hard work."

On the way home, their precious treasure trove of memories was already being opened and enjoyed. And once more the whole group begin happily trading "remember whens."

They were still doing it as the station wagon crossed the George Washington Bridge and headed at last toward the welcoming lights of Manhattan.